SUPERMAN™

BATTLES THE BILLIONAIRE BULLY

written by
MATTHEW K. MANNING

illustrated by
ETHEN BEAVERS

SUPERMAN created by
JERRY SIEGEL & JOE SHUSTER
by special arrangement with
the JERRY SIEGEL FAMILY

raintree
a Capstone company — publishers for children

Raintree is an imprint of Capstone Global Library Limited, a company incorporated in England and Wales having its registered office at 7 Pilgrim Street, London, EC4V 6LB – Registered company number: 6695582

www.raintree.co.uk
myorders@raintree.co.uk

Editor: Anna Butzer
Art Director: Bob Lentz
Graphic Designer: Hilary Wacholz

ISBN 978 1 4747 3750 0
21 20 19 18 17
10 9 8 7 6 5 4 3 2 1

British Library Cataloguing in Publication Data
A full catalogue record for this book is available from the British Library.

Printed in China.

Contents

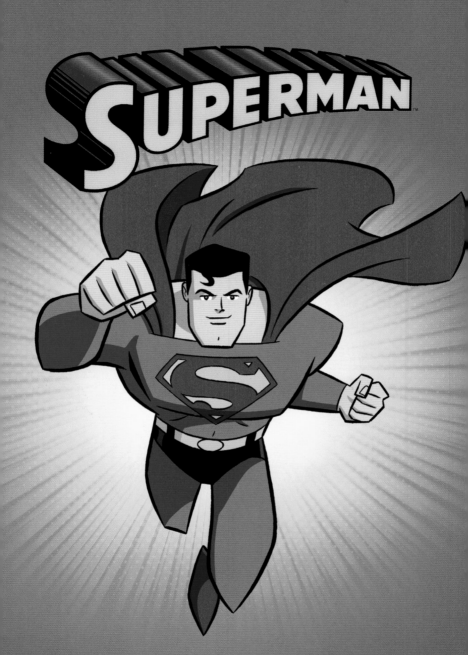

REAL NAME: Kal-El/Clark Kent

ROLE: Super hero and reporter

BASE: Metropolis

HEIGHT: 1.91m (6' 3")

EYES: Blue

HAIR: Black

ABILITIES: Fuelled by the solar radiation of Earth's yellow Sun, Superman's superpowers include: invulnerability, flight, heat vision, X-ray vision, super-strength and super-speed.

BACKGROUND: Years ago in a distant galaxy, the planet Krypton exploded. Its only survivor was a baby named Kal-El who escaped in a rocket ship. After landing on Earth, he was adopted by the Kents, a kind couple who named him Clark. The boy soon discovered he had extraordinary abilities. He chose to use these powers to help others.

CHAPTER 1

THE MAN WITH THE MONEY

The Sun rises over the city of Metropolis. Although there is not a cloud in the sky, one seems to hang over the famous Daily Planet Building.

That dark cloud has a name: Lex Luthor.

DING!

"Who is responsible for this nonsense?!" Lex yells as he exits the Daily Planet Building's lift.

The buzzing newsroom grows silent as all heads turn towards the famous billionaire. Lex doesn't flinch. He's used to people staring when he walks by. He storms into the room with an angry scowl on his face. He brushes by Jimmy Olsen so quickly that he nearly knocks the stack of papers out of the young photographer's hands.

"Don't look now, Lois," Clark Kent whispers, "but here comes trouble."

"That's odd," replies Lois Lane, Clark's friend and fellow reporter, "I didn't think we'd see Lex in here until tomorrow."

SMACK!

"This was you, wasn't it, Kent?" Lex says as he slaps a piece of paper down on Clark Kent's desk. "You think you can print lies like this and get away with it?"

"The better question, Lex," says Lois, "is how you've managed to get a copy of that article. It doesn't see print until tomorrow's paper."

"Not to mention that everything I wrote is true," says Clark. "You're trying to make Kryptonite, Lex. And you're bringing illegal and dangerous materials into the city to do it."

"You listen to me," says Lex. "And listen carefully. If you print this, I'll have you fired."

"Is that so?" Clark calmly replies.

"You think I'm breaking the law now? Wait until you see what I can really do," Lex snarls. "I'll own the *Daily Planet* by the end of this. Are we clear?"

"I think you made your point," says Clark.

"He thinks he can push anyone around just because he has money," says Lois. "I'd like to see him try that with Superman."

He just did, thinks Clark. But he doesn't say anything.

CHAPTER 2

THE LAST SON OF KRYPTON

Like most of the world, Lois doesn't know what Clark Kent does after he leaves the *Daily Planet*. She doesn't know that he heads to the sky in a red cape, fighting super-villains and saving lives. She doesn't know that he is Superman, the world's mightiest hero. And she doesn't know that Clark's past is full of people just like Lex Luthor.

Clark grew up in Smallville, a tiny town in the centre of farmland in Kansas, USA. To his neighbours, he was a bookish, quiet little boy. He never caused any trouble. He always handed in his homework on time.

He never complained about his chores on the family farm. But to his parents, Jonathan and Martha Kent, Clark was something else altogether. He was extraordinary.

Clark is really Kal-El, the last survivor of
the planet Krypton. Earth's yellow Sun gives
him powers far beyond that of a normal
human. Clark is super-strong, super-fast,
has heat and X-ray vision, and can even
fly. What's more, his skin is as strong as
steel, making trips to the doctor all the
more difficult.

CHAPTER 3

THE BOY OF STEEL

In order to protect himself and his family, Clark was forced to keep those fantastic powers to himself. If anyone found out what he could do, it could cause him to be even more of an outcast than he already was. And worse, it could put his innocent parents in danger from those who fear what they don't understand.

That meant Clark had to quit the running team when he could outrace his opponents by a dozen laps. It meant he had to pretend he was unable to do a single pull-up in gym class. And it meant he was forced to turn down an after-school game of American football when his powerful grip popped the ball.

Clark had to hide who he truly was. If he didn't, he would accidentally hurt many of his classmates.

Luckily, most of the kids at Smallville High accepted Clark. They didn't always understand some of the odd things that happened around him. But they accepted him just the same.

But Billy Brandon wasn't most kids. He saw Clark as an easy target. And Billy wasn't happy unless he was taking the easy route.

He would knock books out of Clark's hands. He would throw wads of paper at Clark from the back of the classroom. He would try to trip Clark when he was walking down the halls. Making Clark feel small made Billy feel big. And Billy wanted nothing more than to be the big man on campus.

"Hand over your lunch money, Kent," Billy would say. Clark couldn't fight back. The smallest shove could send Billy through the wall. He couldn't even let Billy hit him. Clark knew that if he did, Billy would break his hand. But Clark had something Billy did not: a sharp wit and X-ray vision.

As Billy threatened him, Clark looked over his shoulder. He narrowed his eyes. He focused his X-ray vision on Billy's locker across the hall.

And as it turned out, Billy had something Clark did not. His locker was full of stolen lunch money and equipment taken from the school's computer lab.

CHAPTER 4

THE REPORTER WITH A PLAN

All it took from Clark was a well-aimed burst of heat vision and some lucky timing. Billy's lock melted to the floor at the perfect moment to catch the eyes of two passing English teachers.

Clark learned that day that there are other ways to fight back. Even if he couldn't use his brawn, he could still use his brain.

Now thinking of Billy Brandon and Lex Luthor, Clark smiles. A lot has changed since his days in Smallville.

But despite what people have told him all of his life, the big city of Metropolis isn't that different. He knows what he has to do.

He opens his email and types a quick message. He attaches a file, and pauses for just a second to think everything over one last time.

Then he hits "send" on his email. *CLICK!*

CHAPTER 5

THE HERO AND THE BULLY

Every computer at the *Daily Planet* has a webcam. Clark had switched on his the moment Lex had approached his desk. With the click of a button, Clark posts his article about Lex's illegal actions on the *Daily Planet* website. He also includes the video footage of Lex's threats. It's time for the whole world to see what type of man Lex Luthor truly is.

And see they do.

It's not exactly Clark Kent who leads the police raid on LexCorp Laboratories. But that fact is not comforting to Lex Luthor.

CRAASH! "It's over, Luthor," Superman says as he bursts into the billionaire's building.

"You didn't think this through did you, alien?" Luthor says. "Always rushing into a room fists first. Even if that room contains your greatest weakness."

Before he spits out his final word, Lex sprints over to the sealed lead container. It holds the artificial Kryptonite.

Superman sees the glowing Kryptonite through the small window of the container. He knows how weak the alien rock makes him. How it saps his powers, leaving him frail and sick. Solely through instinct, Superman pauses for just a moment.

But in that moment, Lex grabs the emergency fire axe mounted on the wall. "I hope you enjoy my work, Superman. I made it for you, after all."

Luthor raises the axe and swings it at the container's window. But it doesn't shatter. *BONK!* The axe simply bounces against the thick, protective plastic.

The only thing that does break is the axe's handle. Superman snaps it over his leg as if it were a twig. *CRAACK!*

"Sorry to disappoint, Lex," Superman says with a grin on his face.

The police escort Lex Luthor out of his building. Captain Maggie Sawyer personally opens the back door of a police car for the corrupt businessman.

"Nice going, Superman," she says. "You caught a big fish this time."

"Thanks, Maggie," Superman replies. "Now if you'll excuse me . . ."

The Man of Steel knows his job isn't done yet. He gives Maggie a quick nod and then rushes back into the building.

WHOOSH!

Moments later, Captain Sawyer watches as Superman takes to the skies, lugging the Kryptonite container behind him.

Safely outside of Earth's atmosphere, Superman spins three times, gaining momentum. Even through the lead container, he can feel the faint sting of the artificial Kryptonite. But it doesn't stop him. The pain just gives him more motivation.

After the third spin, he lets go. *ZOOM!*

The Kryptonite shoots into space on a direct collision course with the Sun.

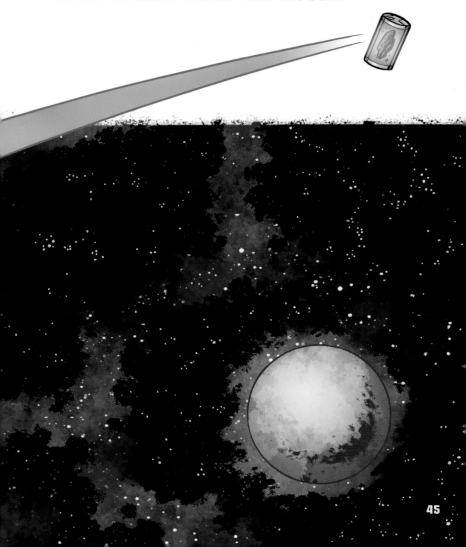

When all is said and done, once again there is not a cloud in the Metropolis sky. There is only a brilliant streak of red and blue. There is only . . .

Superman!

LEX LUTHOR

REAL NAME: Lex Luthor

ROLE: Evil mastermind

BASE: Metropolis

HEIGHT: 1.88m (6' 2")

EYES: Green

HAIR: None

ABILITIES: Possesses a genius level of intelligence. Can quickly master new equipment. He is also a skilled fighter and is fuelled by extreme rage.

BACKGROUND: Lex Luthor is one of the richest and most powerful people in all of Metropolis. He's known as a successful businessman to most, but Superman knows Luthor's dirty little secret – most of his wealth is ill-gotten, and behind the scenes he is a criminal mastermind.

Superman has stopped many of Luthor's evil schemes, but Lex is careful to avoid getting caught red-handed. Lex wants to control Superman to strengthen his grip on Metropolis, but the Man of Steel is not affected by Luthor's power.

Even though Lex Luthor doesn't have superpowers of his own, he is a scientific genius. He has often summoned the help of super-villains in his mission to defeat Superman.

GLOSSARY

bookish when someone is interested in reading books and studying

brawn muscular strength

collision when two things run into each other

momentum amount of force in a moving object determined by the object's mass and speed

outcast someone who is not accepted by other people

raid sudden, surprise attack

scowl to make a frowning expression

wit ability to say clever and funny things

About the author

Matthew K. Manning is the author of over 50 books. He has contributed to many comic books as well, including *Teenage Mutant Ninja Turtles: Amazing Adventures*, *Beware the Batman* and the crossover miniseries *Batman/TMNT Adventures*. He currently resides in Asheville, North Carolina, USA, with his wife Dorothy and their two daughters, Lillian and Gwendolyn. Visit him online at www.matthewkmanning.com.

About the illustrator

Ethen Beavers is a professional comic book artist from Modesto, California, USA. His best-known works for DC Comics include *Justice League Unlimited* and *Legion of Superheroes in the 31st Century*. He has also illustrated for other top publishers, including Marvel, Dark Horse and Abrams.

WRITING PROMPTS

1. Superman uses his powers to protect people and stop villains. Imagine if you were a super hero. What would your superpowers be? What would you do with them? Write about it.

2. Who is a real life super hero to you? Write about this person and explain why you think he or she has super qualities.

3. Clark Kent knows that Lex Luthor is doing something wrong and wants to stop him. Have you ever had to stop someone who was doing something they shouldn't? Write about what happened.

DISCUSSION QUESTIONS

1. Clark realizes he can use his brain to fight back instead of his brawn. What does this mean?

2. Superman keeps his real identity hidden. If you were a super hero how would you keep your identity a secret?

3. This book uses illustrations to help tell the story. Which illustration do you think helps the reader understand the action the most? Why?